MY HEART

My Gift

Corrissa James

Inkwell International

Laurel, NE 68745

www.inkwellinternational.com

MY HEART

My Gift

Chapter One

Serafina Anderson stood by the baggage claim in Omaha's airport, looking for her cousin Trish Cassidy. *Trish James*, she corrected herself. She hadn't seen her cousin since the funeral for Trish's parents almost a decade ago. She wouldn't be here now if she hadn't created such a mess back home in St. Louis.

"Feeny? Is that really you?"

Sera grimaced at the nickname, but turned to see Trish, her arms spread open wide. Her cousin pulled her into a hug, and Sera noticed the talk hulking man watching them. He would have been intimidating if it weren't for the toothy grin plastered on his face.

"It's Sera, now."

Trish stepped back to look at her, still clutching her shoulders. "Now don't you get all high and mighty just because you're a college girl. You'll always be Feeny to me."

Sera scowled, ready to argue the point, but the hulking man stepped forward, one hand extended.

"Hi, Sera. I'm Dalton." As they shook hands, he leaned down to whisper, "Don't worry. I'll work on her for you." He winked, then glanced at Trish, an innocent look on his face. "So, have your bags come through yet?"

"Bags?" Sera rolled her eyes. "I'm only here for the holidays—and just while the dorms are closed."

Dalton glanced at the carry-on at her feet. "If you mean to tell me that you packed everything you needed for the next two weeks in that bag, then you need to give my wife some serious lessons."

Trish slapped her husband's shoulder playfully. "Oh, hush, and grab her bag." She hooked her elbow in Sera's and led her toward the exit. "We have a lot to catch up on, but first I want to know what's up with this?" She tugged on Sera's long black ponytail.

"It's a ponytail. By the way, did you know that there is a ponytail equation? Learned about it in physics. They use it to predict the shape of the ponytail."

"Hardy-har-har, missy. I meant the blue streak. You turning into a smurf or something?"

Sera shrugged. "I think they save transmutation for grad school."

"I'm sure your mother was mortified by your color choice."

Sera nodded, trying to hide a smile. "I'm sure she will be, when she sees it."

"Why, Feeny, you little rebel you. Next you'll be telling me you got a tattoo—oh, no! You didn't?!"

Sera ducked her head and slid in front of her cousin to walk through the exit. They hurried across the drop-off lane, bracing themselves against the icy December wind. Once they were all piled in the truck and Dalton had the heat blasting, Trish studied Sera for a moment.

"I just can't believe it. My innocent little cousin— Feeny the do-gooder, who never broke any rules— has become a rebel."

"I was nine! Nine-year-olds don't break rules."

Dalton snorted. "Clearly you don't know many nine-year-olds."

Trish shook her head, then winked at Sera. "College looks good on you."

Sera mumbled "thanks" as she shifted in her seat.

Dalton gave Sera a sympathetic smile as he whispered, "She'll stop talking. Eventually." He glanced at Trish and smiled, then looked back at Sera. "Probably about the time you get on the plane headed back home."

"Oh, you'll pay for that, Mr. James."

"I hope so, Mrs. James."

Sera pretended to laugh at their obvious teasing, but inside she was groaning. She hadn't planned to come to Nebraska for winter break, but then her best friend started dating some guy from her Spanish class and Sera had realized she couldn't spend the entire break listening to their gooey lovespeak. Trish and Dalton had been married for several months already. Weren't they supposed to be beyond all this romantic crap?

Luckily Sera was able to steer the conversation to Trish's life, so for the next few hours her cousin told her all about how she and Dalton met and how they were building a state-of-the-art horse training facility. Her cousin certainly seemed happy with her life, but Sera couldn't understand how anyone could live in a small town—or the country, for that matter—without going crazy from boredom. She wasn't sure she'd be able to last two weeks. Then again, she didn't have much choice.

Things would have been so much easier if her parents hadn't decided to go to Rome for Christmas. She could have gone home, faced the music, and then figured out what to do next. But Rome had been on her mother's bucket list for as long as Sera could remember. She wouldn't ruin that dream. When the plans with her best friend fell through, Sera had been hard pressed to find an appropriate alternative. Then she remembered hearing about Trish's whirlwind courtship and latched on to the idea of visiting Nebraska for the holidays. At least the three-hour drive to the house passed quickly, which Sera decided was a good omen.

Two weeks. Fourteen days. Surely she could last that long without getting too bored and screwing everything up? She hoped so.

When they pulled into the lane that led to the two-story farmhouse, Sera felt her determination falter. For some reason she'd pictured the farm on the edge of a small town, not twenty minutes away from any hint of civilization. The land that stretched out before them was certainly pretty, especially with the light dusting of snow over everything, but pretty would only last so long.

As they got out of the truck, another truck pulled up behind them, and two men got out. The taller of the two walked up to them with a slight smile on his face.

"Afternoon, boss, Mrs. James." He nodded first at Dalton, then Trish.

Dalton sighed dramatically. "How many times do I have to tell you? I'm not your boss."

The man shrugged. "Sorry, boss. Habit."

"Lucas, you and—is that you Andrew?" Trish stood on her tiptoes to look over Lucas's shoulder.

"You and your brother come inside and have some hot chocolate with us. It's too cold to stand out here any longer."

"That's okay, Mrs. James. We'll only be..."

One withering look from Trish and Lucas was signaling to Andrew to head inside with them. Sera pretended to cough to hide her laugh. Once inside, Trish directed Dalton to take Sera's bag upstairs while she ushered Lucas, Andrew, and Sera into the kitchen.

"Guess we know who wears the pants in this household," Andrew mumbled, earning him a glare from Lucas that would have frightened Sera if she weren't so busy giggling.

They were just sitting down in the kitchen when Dalton reappeared. "So, Lucas, surprised to see you here. Didn't think my sister would give you any time off."

"She runs a tight schedule."

Dalton erupted into laughter, startling all of them except Trish, who was warming the milk for the hot chocolate.

"But we're actually here about Andrew."

Sera saw the dark look flash across Dalton's face, and she turned to study the other man. Andrew's dark brown hair and bright blue eyes contrasted with Lucas's green eyes and auburn hair. She wondered what the quiet Andrew could have done to cause Dalton's reaction, then remembered the comment in the hallway. Such comments could easily be construed as rude. Was Dalton really the kind of man to be offended when people didn't follow the rules of society?

Sera was grateful when Trish set several mugs of hot chocolate on the table. The sweet chocolate offered her an escape from the tension, if only a brief one.

"You boys can talk business later. Right now, I want you to meet my cousin Sera, from St. Louis by way of Chicago. She's a freshman in college who'll be spending Christmas with us. Sera, this is Lucas and Andrew Clark."

Andrew fingered the mug of chocolate, not looking up at Sera. "Another big city girl come to visit us uneducated rural folk?"

Sera saw the hint of a smile tugging at his lips and realized at the last minute that he was teasing her. She was about to make a similarly sarcastic remark when she noticed Lucas glaring at his brother, his lips forming a tight straight line.

Andrew must have realized his mistake because he glanced up, saw Lucas's anger, then looked around to everyone else, finally settling on Sera. "Sorry, I, uh—that didn't sound the way I meant it."

Sera shrugged. "I'll just chalk it up to the cold weather."

"Ha! You think this is cold, just wait."

"Yeah, it gets pretty cold in Chicago, too."

Andrew responded with a dismissive "bah."

"Wait, do you really think it gets colder here than in Chicago?"

"Well, you gotta deal with all the wind here. That's a cold that settles into your bones."

Sera propped her chin up on her fist. "Huh. And me living in Chicago—you think I don't know anything about wind?"

"Not like here."

Lucas interjected into their conversation, his voice so low that Sera almost didn't hear what he said. "Are you really that dense?" When Andrew frowned, the anger making his eyes an even brighter blue, Lucas shook his head. "You think they call it 'The Windy City' because of a few breezes?"

Andrew rubbed his thumb back and forth along the edge of his mug, and Sera could see him struggling to remain calm.

"Actually, with all the buildings, I rarely ever feel the wind anyway." She shrugged. "Unless I'm by the lake."

"Well, you'll feel the wind here, I'm sure." Trish stood, signaling to the mugs on the table. "Anyone need a refresher?"

"No, ma'am, I think we just better say our piece and be on our way before my brother here manages to insult anybody else." Lucas cleared his throat. "I feel bad about leaving you in a bind, what with going to work for your sister and all. But Andrew here still has a debt to work off—he did his time and all, but I believe he has a karmic debt to you. So he'd like to offer his services to you whenever you need him."

Dalton eyed Andrew for a moment, then spoke to Lucas. "That's awfully kind of you to offer, Lucas—"

"Because we could sure use the help."

Everyone but Dalton looked at Trish, who was standing behind her husband, her hand on his shoulder. Only Sera seemed to notice how deeply her hand was digging into his shoulder. Dalton's brow was so furrowed that his face was turning a mottled red.

Trish forced a smiled. "Lucas, why don't you take him for a quick tour of the place. Take Sera, too. I'm sure she'd like to see the horses."

Lucas scrambled to his feet, and Sera and Andrew were quick to follow suit. She was just pulling the front door closed behind her when she heard Dalton's voice from the kitchen, exploding in anger. She slammed the door, mumbling, "I guess the honeymoon's over." She raced down the steps to catch up to Lucas and Andrew.

Lucas was storming ahead of Andrew, glancing over his shoulder every once in a while to throw out another angry comment. "I can't believe you. What in the hell is wrong with you? When did you get to be so stupid? And being snide to someone you just met?"

"He wasn't snide to me."

The two men stopped and turned to Sera, as if just noticing that she was with them.

"That's kind of you to say, Miss Sera, but we both know my brother could use a lesson or two in manners."

Lucas continued walking to the barn, but Andrew hung back.

"I can fight my own fights. And I don't need a college education to do it." He stared at Sera, as if waiting for her to contradict him, then rolled his eyes and turned to follow his brother.

Sera stared after them, a series of retorts racing through her mind, none of which would be considered polite in any context.

Chapter Two

Andrew Clark was kicking himself as he followed his brother into the barn. *And I don't need a college education to do it.* What was wrong with him? He needed the work at the James ranch. Hell, he needed any work he could get. Paying the fines for his legal troubles over the summer had taken a toll on his bank account, and not many people were willing to hire him. None, in fact, save Trish James. And so what did he go and do to thank her? Insult her cousin. Repeatedly. He told himself that it was because Christmas was just a week away.

He hated the holidays. He hated seeing everyone pretending to be so happy, forgetting about all their problems while racking up more and more debt to provide the best gift money could buy. That wasn't the way Christmas was supposed to be. Now he was letting his frustration interfere with his promise to be on his best behavior. Sera didn't seem to mind, though. Did she get his sense of humor when others didn't? He tried to shake the thought from his head. No one got him. Not anymore.

Lucas was pointing out where everything was in the barn. He'd been the main horse trainer for the Jameses until Dalton's sister, Miranda James, convinced him to work on her ranch. Andrew still wasn't sure how that all worked out, but his older brother seemed happy for the first time in a long, long time, so Andrew wasn't going to mess that up. In fact, everyone in his family was suddenly happy—Susannah, Jonathan, Daniel, and now Lucas—all having found someone to keep them warm during the long winter nights. Andrew nodded with each new piece of information Lucas shared, trying to think about how long it had been since someone had shared his bed.

Lucas paused when Sera walked in, and Andrew gave her a tight smile, hoping she wouldn't be too furious with him while he tried to figure out an apology that wouldn't sound stupid. He was surprised when she grinned back.

"I hope you don't mind if I listen in." She looked from Lucas to Andrew and back again. "I've just never seen the behind-the-scenes workings on a farm."

"Ranch." The correction was out before Andrew could stop himself.

"Oh, oops. Right, ranch." Sera grimaced. "Is the neon sign screaming 'dumb city girl' turned on yet?"

"Don't do that."

Lucas and Sera both looked at Andrew, who was frowning.

"Excuse me?" Sera sputtered.

"Don't do that—call yourself dumb."

"Oh, so only you can call me dumb? Is that how it is?"

Lucas stepped between Sera and Andrew, holding up a finger to Sera. "Hold up." He spun around to face Andrew. "Do not tell me that you called her dumb."

Lucas spoke under his breath, but Andrew had no doubts that Sera heard every word, especially when she bit her bottom lip. He had the distinct impression that she was trying not to laugh.

"I didn't." He looked over Lucas's shoulder to Sera. "I didn't call you that."

Sera crossed her arms and stuck out her chin as if she was offended, but he could see the playfulness in her eyes. He braced himself, expecting the worst, suddenly more worried what she would say than what Lucas might do to him.

"Well, I suppose you never used that actual word." She paused, then looked directly at Andrew. "But it was most certainly implied."

"Says who?"

"Says me! And I am the one in college, after all."

She was nearly laughing now, but she couldn't see the anger on Lucas's face, now that he'd had his suspicions confirmed. Andrew took a step back from his brother. Sera had no idea how far she was pushing Lucas. If pushed too far, he could lose control, which could be deadly.

"Lucas, she's joking. It's a joke."

But Lucas wasn't responding. His face was a mask of calm, only his eyes showing the true depth of his anger, although they weren't seeing anything in the here and now. It was a look that Andrew recognized, although it had been years since he'd last seen it. He slowly side-stepped around Lucas, trying to keep his eyes on his brother without looking at him directly. Once past him, he waved at Sera to leave the barn, but she just stood there, the laughing grin still firmly in place.

He grabbed her elbow and pulled her along, slapping his hand over her mouth to keep her from screaming. "Now you really are being dumb," he hissed as he pulled her outside the barn.

He walked for several yards while she struggled against him. If Dalton and Trish happened to see them now, it would not look good at all, so instead of heading for the house, he turned and walked to the far end of the barn. When he finally let her go, all traces of laughter were gone from her face.

"What the hell do you think you're doing?"

"Keep it down! You're going to trigger him."

She started to argue, then snapped her mouth shut and took a step back. After a moment, she asked, "Trigger him?"

"PTSD. He fought in Afghanistan." Andrew peered around the edge of the barn but saw no sign of his brother or the Jameses. When he looked back at Sera, she was chewing on her lip again, this time lost in thought. He reached out to lead her by the elbow, but she jerked away from him. He held up both hands in surrender, then nodded toward a log bench a few yards away. He walked past her slowly, still holding his hands up. He brushed off the snow on the bench, then sat down, patting the place next to him.

She remained standing. "So what do we do now?"

"Wait."

"Until?"

"In a few minutes he'll snap out of it. Then we'll be fine."

Sera leaned against the bench. "Is he dangerous?"

"No." His response was curt, and Sera flinched.

"Jeez, okay. Sorry. I don't know anything about PTSD."

"Don't they teach you anything useful in college?"

"PTSD would be covered in the psych program. I couldn't get into it."

They were both silent for several moments. Andrew was trying to figure out what to say that wouldn't make him sound like a jerk, but everything that popped into his head sounded increasingly arrogant to him.

"Is he your only brother?"

"Nope."

They fell into silence again. He told himself to tell her about his family, but something stopped him. It was as if he was afraid that, if she found out about them, she'd immediately fall into their way of thinking that he was worthless—which was about the dumbest thought he'd ever had, and he'd had some doozies in his life. Still, he couldn't shake the feeling that it was important for her not to find out too much about his family. At least not right now.

"Well, golly, Mr. Rancher, sir, this has sure been fun."

Andrew couldn't help but smile. "Yeah, I'm not the greatest conversationalist, huh?"

"Uh, no, you won't be winning any awards in that category any time soon."

"Maybe I outta go to one of them hoity-toity schools in the city." In his head, it sounded funny, cute even. Once he said it out loud, he wanted to walk back into the barn and tell Lucas to smack him around a bit.

Sera twirled and sat on the bench in one fluid moment. "Why do you do that?"

He shrugged, wondering why she wasn't mad at him for such a remark.

"I mean, really—are the people around here who went to college such jerks that you think that college is a joke?"

Andrew thought for a moment, then laughed. "Yeah, actually. Pretty much. They go away normal kids and all, then come back and think they have the solution to every problem known to man."

"So, I take it you were one of the smart ones?" She leaned over to nudge his shoulder with hers. "Skip college and go straight to work?"

"Sure, I guess so. I've been working the farm for as long as I can remember."

"Ranch."

He shook his head. "Nope, farm. My family has a farm. This is a ranch."

"So why are you working here and not on your farm?"

Andrew glanced around, not sure how much he wanted to tell her. "I got into some trouble this summer."

She turned to face him. "Oh, do tell!"

He scratched his head. She seemed almost excited to learn that he was a trouble-maker. "Just a little vandalism, cutting of fences and the like."

"Oh." She kicked at the fluff of snow on the ground.

He cleared his throat. "Dalton's fences." The brilliant smile she gave him nearly bowled him over.

"That explains his reaction." She waved toward the house. "But why his fences?"

"Yeah, I thought he—well, his sister—was stealing our cattle."

The corner of her mouth twitched. "So…cattle rustling?"

"Yes. Cattle rustling. Which is a big deal. Cows ain't cheap, you know."

She shook her head, her ponytail sweeping back and forth. Andrew fought the urge to reach out and stop it from moving. "No, I don't know."

"Right, because you didn't grow up on a farm. I did, so I know all this stuff—without having to go to college."

"Sure. Why waste all that time and money taking useless classes on stuff you'll never need out in the real world, paying professors to rake you over the coals?"

He glanced at her from the corner of his eye. "Why do I think we're no longer talking about me?"

Sera sat up straight. "Huh? No, no. I'm a huge proponent of college. It's more than just the classes. It's the whole learning experience."

He stared at her for a moment, trying to understand the sudden shift in her demeanor. It was like she was no longer talking to him but rather reciting something she'd be trained to say. Finally, he shrugged.

"If you say so, but I can get all the learning experiences I need working the farm. I don't need to pay someone to teach me anything, and somehow I don't think some professor in a tweed jacket, smoking a pipe is gonna be able to teach me how to rope a stray calf or know when one of the best breeders might be sick. Those are just things you learn natural, in the field, so to speak."

She stared at him, wide eyed. "Tweed jacket? Pipe? You really have an outdated perception of college life."

"Did you just call me old?" He feigned offense.

"I think I did." Sera crossed her arms and smiled, clearly proud with herself. "I guess now we're even. I'm dumb, you're old."

Andrew frowned. "I didn't call you dumb, and I told you not to call yourself that."

"But you just said that people who go to college are wasting their time and money, which I think we can both agree is pretty dumb."

Andrew jumped to his feet. "Say whatever you want, kid. But stop saying you're dumb. It's really an ugly habit."

Sera clasped one hand to heart, as if she'd been shot, then stood up slowly. "Oh, so I'm not dumb, but I'm ugly? Gee, thanks."

Andrew clenched his fists and looked up into the sky. He counted to three, then stepped back from her, bowing slightly. "Whatever. Say whatever you want, Miss Higher Education. Clearly I don't have the brains to argue with you."

Andrew turned to walk away and ran right into Lucas.

"I think it's time for you to wait in the truck, brother."

Andrew stormed past his brother. "I couldn't agree more!"

Chapter Three

Sera sat hunched over her coffee cup, willing the caffeine to give her at least a little energy. This was her second cup, and so far it wasn't helping much. For the first time in months she could sleep as much as she wanted to without worrying about homework she didn't understand or exams she wasn't prepared for, but instead of spending ten hours lost in the splendor of dreamland, she'd spent the night tossing and turning. She told herself she was still worried about breaking her news to her parents and how heartbroken they would be. Heartbroken or devastated, she wasn't sure which. Maybe both. Except her thoughts continuously turned to Andrew Clark and what a jerk he'd been.

The really crazy part was that she wasn't offended in the least by his comments. Rather, she found it all very amusing—mostly because she recognized that he was trying to be sociable. Awkwardly so, but sociable nonetheless.

She shuddered. If that was sociable, she'd hate to see him when he was angry and willfully trying to inflict harm on someone.

"Good morning, Feeny!"

Sera groaned. Her cousin was too chipper by far. Chipperness when the sun was just rising was wrong on so many levels. Trish scooped dog food into a bowl for Traitor, their black lab, then dropped into the seat across from Sera, a steaming mug in her hands.

"Sweetie, you don't look too good. Was the bed not comfortable? Do you need more blankets?"

"Don't worry, I'm fine. The bed's fine, the blankets are fine. Everything's fine."

Trish arched an eyebrow at her cousin, then set her mug down and folded her arms on the table. "Four fines? I don't think so. What's wrong?"

Sera brushed her hair back and sat up. "Nothing. I guess my brain just hasn't caught on yet that I'm on break."

"Ah." Trish nodded. "I remember those days. Man, I miss school sometimes—not the tests, mind you. Those sucked. But the constant learning. It's just...invigorating, right?"

"Mm-hmm." Sera sipped on her coffee, hoping Trish got the hint and changed the subject.

"So your mom said you're studying psychology. That's gotta be fun, delving into the human mind and all?"

Sera choked on her coffee. "Sure. I guess." She considered correcting her cousin, but as Trish continued to eye her, Sera glanced around the kitchen, uncomfortable under such scrutiny. She was grateful when Traitor came over for some attention. She rubbed his head and ears until he flopped over onto his back, exposing his belly for more rubs.

"Traitor," Trish mumbled. "Your name suits you."

"So why don't you have any decorations up yet?" Sera finally glanced back at Trish. "You do know it's Christmas in like four days, right?"

"You don't say?" Trish tried to keep a straight face, but her giggles almost made her spill her coffee. "Actually, I was waiting for you to get here. Dalton's not big on holidays, so I thought you and I could try sprucing the place up a bit."

"Sure. Sounds fun. On one condition."

"Name it."

"Sometime before Christmas Eve we get to bake cookies—the real homemade kind, not the store-bought stuff."

Trish smiled. "I think that can be arranged."

Dalton stumbled through the kitchen door, a sheepish grin spreading across his face when he saw the two women at the table. He glanced at them, fully dressed, then down at himself, wearing only pajama bottoms. "Morning." He poured himself a cup of coffee before sitting down with the women. "Sorry, I'm not used to house guests."

Sera laughed. "Co-ed dorm. Trust me, I've seen a lot worse."

Dalton frowned. "I think I should be offended by that. I'll let you know after I've had my coffee."

"Well, drink up quick, hon, because we need to go find a Christmas tree today."

Dalton slurped at his coffee while nodding his head. "I know exactly where they are. Hardware store's got a whole bunch of them."

Trish looked at Sera and rolled her eyes. "Men." She patted Dalton's hand. "No, silly. We want a live tree."

Dalton groaned, but Trish ignored him.

"I've been checking out some contenders on the ranch, over by the creek."

"The creek? Why didn't you say so?" Dalton leaned over to nuzzle his wife's neck. "Perhaps we can go for a dip while we're there?"

Trish gave Sera a bewildered look. "Seriously, men. They're all alike, am I right?" She pushed Dalton away. "Listen, if you want to go dip your nether regions in that ice-cold creek, be my guest. Maybe then I could get some sleep at night."

Sera tried not to laugh as she watched Dalton processing the information, but when he shuddered uncontrollably, she couldn't hold it back any longer. He hugged his arms across his chest, rubbing his biceps to warm up.

Trish stood up and hauled Dalton to his feet. "Tell you what. You go put on some clothes instead of traipsing around here half naked, and we'll make breakfast."

He gave her a quick peck on the cheek. "Biscuits and gravy?"

"Sure, just get going—and take Traitor with you. We don't need his big puppy dog eyes staring at us while we cook."

By the time they cleaned up, the sun was high above the horizon, and Trish found Sera some heavy gloves, a thick scarf, and a knitted hat. She stood back to survey the results, then pulled the hat down further and scarf up higher until only a thin swath of skin was visible.

"I'm not gonna be the one to tell your parents you caught pneumonia while you were here. Your daddy would tan my hide."

Sera pulled down the scarf to talk. "And you think he'll be okay with suffocating me?"

"You'll thank me for it."

They headed out toward the barn, where Dalton was standing next to two four-wheelers. When he saw the women, he called to Andrew, who appeared from the barn. Before Sera understood what was happening, Trish and Dalton were on one of the four-wheelers, heading out toward the hills. Andrew sat on the other, waiting for Sera.

She remembered how anxious he'd been to get away from her yesterday, and then the thoughts that plagued her all night came rushing back to her. "You know, you don't need to go with us—I mean, if you have other work to do."

Andrew glanced over his shoulder at her, then shrugged. He swung off the four-wheeler. "You know how to run one, city girl?" He nodded at the four-wheeler.

She rolled her eyes. "Of course. We have four-wheelers in the city, you know." She had never actually ridden on one, but she wasn't going to tell him that. She threw her leg over the seat and pulled herself close to the handlebars. She turned the key, then pressed the start button.

Nothing happened.

"You got it in neutral?"

She pretended to fidget with the knobs. "Yep."

"You sure?"

"Okay, fine, so I've never ridden one, but how hard can it be?"

Andrew shook his head. "Not hard. A college kid like yourself ought to be able to learn." He climbed on the back and wrapped his arms around her so he could reach the various knobs. "Ignition, starter, choke." He pointed to the various knobs.

"Check." She was surprised by how normal her voice sounded, considering his proximity.

He pointed down to a lever by her foot. "Gear shifter."

"Ah, there you are, you little devil."

"Hook your foot under it and pull up to move up the gears. Push down to return to first. Neutral's between first and second."

"Got it." She waited for him to get off, but he didn't move.

"What are you waiting for? Christmas?" He chuckled at his own joke.

Sera groaned. "I thought you were just going to teach me."

"I am. That was the intro lesson. Now we'll take it out for a spin, see if you can pass the test."

Sera's body jerked as she tensed.

Andrew pulled his hands back. "Whoa, easy there, girl."

She knew his quiet words were meant to calm her down, that there was no maliciousness in them at all, but she couldn't stop herself from reacting. She slid off the four-wheeler, but before she could walk away, he grabbed her elbow.

"You know, this is stupid. I don't need to learn to ride this piece of junk. It's not like we ride these things in the city, anyway." She tugged at her arm, trying to escape his grasp, but he wouldn't let go. She looked away, refusing to let him see the tears welling up in her eyes.

Andrew let out a low whistle. "Wow. Spoiled much, brat?"

Sera whipped around on him, feeling as if she'd just been punched and was ready to do some punching of her own. But he was smiling at her, a genuine smile that lit up his entire face. He tugged on her arm, more gently this time, and Sera let herself be maneuvered back onto the four-wheeler.

"Sorry," she mumbled. "I don't like tests."

"So I gathered." He rested his chin on her shoulder. "Don't think of it as a test. Think of it as springing the hired help from the tedious chore of mucking out the horse stalls."

She giggled. "Pretty bad, huh?"

"Definitely not as fun as four-wheeling."

He walked her through the process again and, after a few stalled attempts, they were finally following after

Dalton and Trish—well, following their fresh tracks in the snow, as the older couple were nowhere to be seen.

They came upon a small pond covered in ice. The other four-wheeler was parked next to it, but Dalton and Trish were nowhere to be found.

Sera parked the four-wheeler and turned it off. She slid off the machine and turned just as Andrew was preparing to yell for Dalton.

"No!" She slapped her hand across his mouth, then—realizing what she'd done—jerked it back. "I mean, Dalton just mentioned having some private time with Trish, and I wouldn't want to...uh...interrupt that, you know?"

Andrew blanched, then let a slow grin spread across his face. "Maybe working for Dalton James won't be so bad after all."

Sera rolled her eyes. "Trish is right: Men!"

"Oh, come on. We're not all bad." He stuck out his tongue at her. "Well, maybe your city men are, but us country guys..."

She turned to walk along the edge of the pond before he could finish, which caused him to burst out laughing. The pond was not that big, a bit bigger than an Olympic-sized swimming pool, if she had to guess. She was about halfway around the pond when she heard something and looked back to see Andrew, reclining on the four-wheeler, whistling.

He certainly was different than any of the men she had ever met. Well, boys really. Andrew was at least five years older than she was, if not more, which was funny considering how many social faux-pas he made. She groaned out loud. "Faux-pas? Really? Maybe I am a snob after all."

"What's that?" Andrew called to her from across the pond.

"Nothing. Just agreeing with you."

He sat up. "About what?"

"Nothing."

"What?"

She waved a hand, telling him to forget it.

"Oh, come on!"

"Fine! Hold on!" She certainly wasn't going to yell across the pond that she was a snob. She didn't think she would even admit it to him. She started to walk back around the pond, then stopped. She stepped out onto the edge of the ice, testing it with her full weight. She took one step out, jumped a little, then shrugged and started walking across the pond.

She heard Andrew yelling at her to stop. *Typical.* Then the icy water shocked her into numbness.

Chapter Four

Andrew alternated between shouting profanities and yelling for Dalton. He knew the pond was much deeper that its size suggested by the way Sera's head bobbed under water. She'd gone into cold shock the second her body hit the icy water. She wasn't trying to pull herself out of the water, but was gasping for air, which could all too easily turn into hyperventilating. If he didn't get her to calm down soon, it wouldn't be the extreme cold that would kill her, but cardiac arrest. His mind cycled through a series of possible outcomes, none of them good, and he gulped in air as if he were the one sinking into the frigid depths.

He grabbed the rope that he had secured to the back of the four-wheeler for hauling the Christmas tree back to the house.

"Sera! Sera! Can you hear me? I need to you to calm down. Slow, even breaths. Can you do that for me?"

He continued calling out to her, keeping his voice as even and authoritative as he could while he tied the rope to a nearby tree. He made a lasso in the other end.

"I'm going to throw you a rope. I need you to catch it. Can you hear me, Sera? Catch the rope."

He circled the rope several times above his head, then flicked it out toward Sera. It landed half in the hole and half on the ice.

"Get the rope, Sera. Do you hear me? Over your head then under your shoulders so I can pull you out."

She didn't grab the rope. Her breathing was becoming increasingly labored. Andrew walked several steps out onto the ice, calling to Sera to grab the rope. He dropped to his stomach and pulled himself along the ice. She was a good twenty feet from him when he realized she was no longer gasping for breath, but forcing herself to inhale slowly.

"Good girl. You're gonna be fine. Now just grab the rope."

He was about five feet from her when she suddenly shot above the surface, her arms extended out and above the ice. When she came back down, her arms landed on the ice. She was trying to pull herself out.

"Yes, just hold on."

She was looking at him, and he was shocked by the lack of fear in her eyes. Instead, he saw concern—for him.

He reached out to grab her hand, propelling himself the last few inches. He wrapped his hand around her wrist, then leveraged his body to pull her up.

He heard the ice cracking all around him. He jerked on her arm with all his might, sending her sprawling onto the ice.

"Don't stop. Crawl to the edge. Go, now!"

He rolled and spun around until he was heading back to shore right behind her. She moved with surprising speed; he almost couldn't keep up. A part of his mind registered pride, but the other part shoved it aside, saying he could be proud of her later. Now they needed to get off the ice.

When they were a few feet from the edge, Andrew stood up and grabbed Sera off the ice, carrying her to the four-wheeler. She wasn't wearing her coat anymore. She must have ditched it when it started pulling her down. *Smart girl.* He stripped off her long-sleeved shirt and tossed it aside, then took off his coat and wrapped it around her. He sat in front of her.

"I need you to hold on to me. Can you do that?"

She wrapped her hands around him.

"Tighter."

She complied.

He started the four-wheeler and raced back toward the house, stopping just in front of the steps leading to the front porch. When he stepped off the four-wheeler, he could feel Sera shaking. Her bones seemed to be rattling from the cold. He carried her up the front steps and into the house.

"You're safe. We'll get you warmed up and laugh about this. Soon. I promise."

He continued cooing to her as he carried her up the stairs. She pointed to a door, and he pushed through it. He set her on the bed, then lifted her feet, pulling off her shoes and thick socks. He stripped off her jeans. She had a small purple heart tattooed near her hip. He fought the urge to stop and examine it and instead pulled the blanket around her, cocooning her in dry warmth. He found extra blankets in the closet and pulled out another one to tuck around her and a third to wrap around her head, pulling her wet hair away from her body as much as he could.

"Andrew?"

"Hmm?" He leaned over her to look in her face. Her eyes were closed, and her cheeks were a light rosy color. She was still shivering, but it was subsiding.

She tried to smile, but it was interrupted by a strong shudder. Then she opened her eyes. "You were right. It is colder here."

"Told you that college education was worthless." He leaned down and brushed a quick kiss across her lips. When he pulled back, he frowned. "That was the coldest kiss ever."

He winked at her, and she giggled in return.

"You okay here for a minute?" He tucked in all the edges of the blanket. "Feeling at least a little better?"

She nodded.

"Okay, then, I'm going to go downstairs and see if I can find you some hot soup."

She nodded, but he still leaned over her.

"Um, don't expect too much, okay?"

"What—no homemade chicken noodle soup? What kind of country boy are you, anyway?"

He winked. "The kind who knows how to make instant soup. Take it or leave it."

Sera closed her eyes. "I supposed it'll have to do."

Andrew stared at her for a few more seconds, suddenly not wanting to leave her. He finally shook his head, then made his way downstairs. She needed to rest, and although his thoughts were quickly becoming quite heated, they were not the kind of warming up she needed. Not right now, at least.

Chapter Five

Sera heard something slam against the entryway wall downstairs, followed by a bellow from Dalton. She scrambled out of the bed, wrapping the blankets around her as best as she could, then shuffled out into the hallway and to the railing so she could look downstairs.

"Get out!" Dalton was gripping the edge of the door, waiting for Andrew to walk through it so he could slam it shut behind him. But Andrew just stood there, facing Dalton, the cup of soup in his hands.

Trish rushed in, glanced at Dalton, then turned to Andrew. "Where's Sera?" Her voice was hoarse with concern.

"I'm up here, Trish."

All three looked up at her, and Sera realized that letting them see her had been a mistake. Dalton's face turned an even deeper shade of red while Trish raced up the stairs.

"Oh, my God. Are you okay? What happened?" Trish tried to pull the blankets tighter around her. Sera waved her away. "You need to get back in bed. Andrew, were you bringing that up here?" She pointed at the cup in his hands.

"Yes, ma'am."

As Sera let her cousin lead her away, she saw Dalton snatch the cup out of Andrew's hands, spilling the hot soup all over himself. She started giggling, which turned into a coughing fit.

"See? Pneumonia. Thank goodness your father's not here." Trish flashed a tight smile at Sera as she helped her back into bed, but the younger girl could see the concern in her eyes. "We saw the rope and your shirt at the pond...well, Dalton was ready to kill Andrew. Then we saw the hole in the ice. What the hell was he thinking?"

"It's okay, Trish. I'm fine." She crawled under the blankets, exhaustion washing over her as the adrenaline of the last hour wore off. "He took care of me."

"He shouldn't have let you on the ice to begin with."

Sera closed her eyes and smiled. "As if I need anyone to 'let' me do anything."

Sera slept the rest of the day and through most of the night, although her sleep was plagued by dreams of a hand reaching out of the sky to pluck her from an avalanche of snow and ice. The hand pulled her up and up, as she dangled in the air, terrified. Yet even in the dream, she understood that she was not afraid of falling, but rather of not reaching whoever was pulling her along. As soon as she realized this, she would wake up, only to fall back into a fitful sleep that eventually returned her to the same dream. The morning sun was just starting to lighten her windows when the hand in the dream finally pulled her into someone's arms and she heard a familiar voice say "city girl" just before she woke up once again. This time she swung out of bed and got dressed before heading downstairs.

Her stomach snarled to life when she smelled the bacon frying. She found Trish alone in the kitchen, cooking enough food to feed all the farmers and ranchers in several counties.

"Hungry?"

"Famished."

Trish handed her a plate of hash browns, eggs, bacon, and toast. Sera shoved a piece of bacon in her mouth as she walked to the table. Her plate was halfway cleaned off when Trish sat down with her, sliding a cup of coffee over to her.

"So how you feeling today?"

"Fine." Sera shrugged. "A little sore but okay. I wasn't really in the water that long."

"That's what Andrew said when I could finally get him to answer the phone."

Sera bit into the toast and cocked her head at Trish.

"Ah, yes. Well, my husband, in his infinite wisdom, fired Andrew."

Sera spat the toast across the table. "He did what?! But Andrew saved me!"

Trish wiped pieces of toast from her blouse, then folded her arms on the table in front of her.

Sera reached across the table to grab her hand. "You have to talk to Dalton, get Andrew his job back."

"Unfortunately, my husband has a stubborn streak that's a mile long."

Sera groaned.

"Which is why I sent him to help his sister today. The last thing we need to ruin our holiday fun is a broody man underfoot, right?"

Sera set her fork down, then wiped her hands on a napkin. "I kinda screwed up the whole Christmas tree outing, didn't I?"

"Meh, no worries." Trish winked. "Nothing a little shopping therapy won't cure."

An hour later, they were heading down the country road in Trish's truck. "I hope you don't mind," Trish said as she turned down a lane. "I invited someone to come along with us. You know, carry our bags and all."

Sera didn't understand until she saw Andrew standing at the end of the lane, his hands shoved in his pockets and a deep frown on his face. He opened the passenger door and waited for Sera to slide into the middle before he swung himself into the cab.

They drove for twenty minutes in silence before Trish pulled into a gas station. Andrew slid out of the truck to pump the gas for her, and when he was done Trish went inside to pay while Sera and Andrew sat in the truck. Sera tried to think of something funny to say to break the tension, but her mind kept offering up the vision from her dream when he was holding her in his arms.

"Guess I was right about who wears the pants in their family." Andrew leaned over to nudge Sera's shoulder with his own. "And I didn't even need a fancy education."

They looked at each other, then burst out laughing.

Sera wiped at the corners of her eyes, trying to dry the tears. "I'll talk to Dalton. Once he understands, I'm sure he'll—"

"Don't need the help of a college girl."

Sera scowled at him. Why shouldn't she help him? It was all her fault, after all. But he had crossed his arms and stuck his nose in the air. She folded her arms across her chest. "Fine. Whatever!"

"Duh. That was a joke."

"Well, it wasn't very funny!"

"Well, clearly!"

They stared at each other, her scowling and him frowning, then burst into laughter once again. They continued staring at each other as their laughter died down, and Sera suddenly thought about kissing him. The thought startled her, but she didn't look away. She wanted him to kiss her, and the look he was giving her made Sera think he wanted the same. She leaned closer, almost imperceptibly so, and parted her lips just enough to let him know that she was ready for a kiss.

"Sorry that took so long," Trish said as she hoisted herself into the truck. "Had to hear the latest gossip." She studied Sera and Andrew, who were doing everything they could not to look at each other. "But I'm guessing there was something much more gossip-worthy happening in here."

Sera glared at her cousin.

Trish started the truck. "Or maybe not."

"Hey, help me out here." Trish motioned for Sera to join her and Andrew at the table next to the coffee kiosk at the mall. "Help me convince old Andrew over here that Christmas is not a horrible holiday."

"Horrible?" Sera dropped several bags on the floor next to them as she sat down and looked at Andrew. "How so?"

He shook his head. "I never said 'horrible.'"

"No, you didn't," Trish said. "I think you said it was a 'commercial charade propped up by a fat man touting crap no one needs.'"

Sera sighed. "Well, that does just about sum it up."

Trish groaned at her while Andrew eyed Sera, his expression hooded.

"Then why are we even bothering with Christmas shopping if the two of you are such bah-humbugs?"

Sera smiled. "Because it's fun."

Trish rolled her eyes. "Did you at least get everything you needed?"

"Almost." She had found a Black Hills gold bracelet for her mother and a money clip for her father. She'd also bought a South Dakota sweatshirt for her best friend. She had brought a hand-crafted glass ornament from Chicago for Trish and Dalton. But she still needed to find something for Andrew. She glanced at the pile of bags next to Trish. "Are you shopping for the entire state?"

Andrew frowned. "Seems like it, doesn't it."

Sera looked between the two of them, confused.

"Mr. Jolly over there is upset that I picked up a few trinkets for his family."

Sera eyed the bags again, then looked at Andrew. "Just how big is your family?"

"Not that big."

"Oh, quit being a poopy head."

Sera tried not to laugh at Andrew's expression of surprise.

"Seriously, you act like I spent a fortune on these little knick-knacks. Excuse me if I think it is common courtesy to provide little gifts for people celebrating Christmas with us this year."

An uneasy feeling came over Sera. This was her first Christmas away from her parents, and she had assumed it would be a quiet affair, with her, Trish, and Dalton. But Andrew and his entire family were coming over for the Christmas Eve party, which apparently would include gift-giving. Certainly she wouldn't be expected to buy gifts for everyone, especially as she didn't even know them. Would she?

When Andrew stood to throw away their empty coffee cups, Sera leaned over to Trish. "Just how big is this event gonna be? I thought you said a small gathering, but—"

"Don't worry." Trish rested her hand on Sera's arm. "It's just the neighbors. And their plus ones. It's our first party together, so I'm not sure how fancy schmancy it will be." She pursed her lips in thought. "But it would be nice to get some of those cowboys out of their dirty old jeans."

"Excuse me?"

Trish laughed. "Oh, you know what I mean." She winked. "Although if you decide to take that more literally..."

Sera crossed her arms in frustration. How had the conversation come back to her again? "I'm sure all those significant others would just love that, eh?"

"Not everyone has a plus one."

"And not everyone needs romance to make life complete."

"You're absolutely right." Trish shrugged. "Then again, if you decided that maybe a little holiday fun is on the agenda..."

They both glanced up as Andrew returned to the table. Trish smiled. "Well, I still need to pick out a little something for Sera's Christmas—seeing as this is her first Christmas away from her parents and all."

Andrew glanced at Sera, and she saw a wave of pain crash in his eyes. She reached out to him. "Oh, it's not like they're dead or anything. Just in Europe."

His blue eyes turned an icy cold that made Sera shiver. When she glanced at Trish, her cousin was wincing.

"Oh, Andrew. I'm so sorry. I had no idea...your parents?"

He shrugged her off and stood. "It was a long time ago." He snatched up all the bags and headed for the door.

Sera dropped her head into her hands. Now she was making as many faux-pas as Andrew, except hers weren't just embarrassing. They also hurt.

Chapter Six

Andrew pushed open the glass doors and welcomed the icy air that made his lungs contract. His parents had died a long time ago—well, nearly ten years ago, but sometimes it only felt like ten days. Christmas was the worst. His parents had loved Christmas, especially his mother, who every year went out of her way to find a meaningful gift for each of her children.

It was the only time Andrew ever felt like someone actually knew him, understood who he was as a person, and liked him.

Now Christmas was just the same as every other day of the year, except he got gifts from his siblings that proved, time and again, that they didn't know him at all. Sitting around the Christmas tree, watching his brothers, sister, and niece unwrap gifts and become all giddy with what they found under the wrapping paper, was the loneliest Andrew ever felt.

But he didn't expect Sera to understand that. How could she? Her parents were still alive, but she chose not to spend Christmas with them.

He stopped at the curb and frowned. Why was that? Why was she here and not in Europe with her parents? Sure she had a streak of rebellion in her, but she didn't seem like the type to shun family. Quite the opposite. She'd decided to come to Nebraska to be with family for Christmas.

Curious, Andrew spun around to head back inside and ran into Sera.

"I'm so sorry. I had no idea. Please, don't be mad at me."

He shook his head. "I'm not mad. Why would you think that?"

"Because." She motioned to the bags. "You grabbed everything and walked out."

He rolled his eyes as he stepped off the curb and headed to the truck. "Might want to get a refund on that college education."

"Seriously?!" Sera yelled after him, then rushed to catch up. "I came out here to check on you, to be nice to you, and you throw college in my face? Again?!"

He laughed as he picked up his pace, forcing her to jog to keep up with his long strides. "Nice? You call yelling at me being nice?" He nodded at an older couple who slowed as they walked toward the mall, interested in the scene unfolding before them. "Yelling at people in a public place—that's what these big city folk consider nice."

The older couple frowned at Sera.

"Are you kidding me?" She stuck her tongue out at the old couple, which caused Andrew to howl with laughter. "I'm glad you find this so amusing, especially given how many times you've stuck your foot in your mouth in the three days I've been here."

Andrew stopped at the truck, set half the bags down, then reached into his pocket for the keys. Except he didn't have the keys. Trish had the keys because they had taken her truck, and Trish was still inside. He closed his eyes, trying to think of some way to get out of this without Sera realizing what he'd done. He had no doubt that she would lord such knowledge over him, teasing him mercilessly. It was what he would do if he were in her shoes, teasing her until she because so frustrated that her cheeks flushed and her eyes burned....

He cleared his throat and straightened his shoulders. Better not to think such thoughts. Not now, not here, when he didn't have a key for the truck and no place to whisk her away to.

Andrew finally turned to Sera, ready to face the music. She was standing just a few feet from him, jumping up and down to keep warm. His eyes narrowed.

"What the hell is wrong with you? Where's your coat?"

"I—"

"Never mind. Get inside before you freeze to death, you crazy girl." He pointed back toward the mall, but when she didn't respond fast enough, he grabbed her hand and started dragging her inside.

"Wait, the bags!"

Andrew swore under his breath. He stopped, dropped the rest of the bags, and stripped off his coat, wrapping it around her shoulders. He pulled at the lapels until she was just a few inches from him, then growled at her. "Woman, I swear to God, if you get sick and die on me because you're too thick headed to stay warm, I'm gonna come find you in the afterlife. Do you understand?"

She nodded slowly.

"Say it!"

"I understand."

Her voice was shaky, but he couldn't tell if it was because she was cold or scared. He pushed her back several feet, then pointed toward the mall once again. She clicked her heels together, then took off running for the mall. He watched her to make sure she went all the way inside before he turned to collect the bags.

He hurried back to the mall and was not at all surprised to find her waiting just inside the door, his coat already removed. He gripped the bags tightly as he confronted her.

"Do you not get what Dalton would do to me if you got sick? Are you sure you're really in college? Because I'm beginning to wonder."

She gave him a lop-sided grin and shrugged, as if that was supposed to explain everything.

"Maybe you should go join your parents in Europe. At least they might have some control over you."

Sera's eyes widened, and her cheeks flushed with anger. Andrew cringed. He'd hit a sore spot without realizing it. There'd be hell to pay now. He braced himself for the impending lashing.

Instead, she burst into tears and threw his coat at him before turning to run through the crowded mall. Andrew stared after her, wishing she had yelled, screamed, cursed—anything but cried. Then maybe he wouldn't be feeling like a complete idiot. He wouldn't be hurting so much, either.

Chapter Seven

Sera spent the rest of the day shopping by herself and avoiding Andrew, although she did find a small gift for him. She knew she shouldn't be upset with him. He had no clue why his words hit so close to home, so why she had run from him crying was beyond her. She'd texted Trish to let her know she would meet them after lunch for the ride home. To Trish's credit, her cousin didn't press for details, just sent back a quick "no problem."

Sera wandered in and out of store after store, trying to lose herself in the sounds of Christmas carols and the smell of roasted pecans from one of the kiosk vendors, but Andrew's words kept coming back to her. *At least they might have some control over you.*

But that was the whole problem. They'd been asserting their control over her entire life, and she'd ended up following a career path that didn't suit her in the least. Instead of facing her parents, she'd basically run away. Now she was stuck preparing for a party that she didn't want to attend, with people she didn't even know. And one person she wished she knew better.

Sera berated herself for letting such thoughts in. She was only here for another ten days, and then she'd probably never return. There was no sense in getting to know anyone better at this point, no matter how good he'd smelled when he pulled her so close in the parking lot.

"Oh, my God. Stop it!"

"Excuse me." A sales clerk stepped up to Sera. "Can I help you, miss?"

Sera let a nervous smile play across her lips. "No, thanks."

The clerk continued to eye her.

Sera finally whispered, "It's the Christmas carols." She pointed toward the ceiling, where she assumed the speakers were hidden. "They make me a little nuts sometimes."

The clerk laughed. "Oh, honey, try working here." She scampered off to another customer.

Sera hurried out of the store, waiting until she was in front of the neighboring store to laugh out loud.

Several shoppers turned to look at her, not stopping as they snaked through the crowds. Sera waved to them. If she was going to go crazy, might as well go big.

"Careful, you're scaring the locals."

The deep voice made her jump, but she recovered—hopefully smoothly enough that he hadn't noticed. One glance up into his blue eyes and she knew she wasn't fooling him, which made her laugh even louder.

She hooked her elbow in his and they continued walking. "I think I might have found my true calling."

"You are pretty good at scaring us."

"Um, yeah. About that."

"I'm not prying. Scout's honor." He held up three fingers. "You don't have to tell me anything."

"Good." She flashed him a grin. "Because I wasn't planning to. So let's go find Trish. I've had about enough of these crowds as I can stand."

"Hallelujah!"

The next day, Sera and Trish took over the kitchen to make Christmas cookies. They started with shortbread, but then moved on to sugar cookies and gingerbread men, decorating the cookies in a multitude of holiday colors.

Just after noon, Dalton sauntered into the kitchen. "I'm guessing we're on our own for lunch today."

Trish tossed him a broken cookie. "We've got a plate of rejects if you want to munch on them."

Dalton popped the cookie in his mouth, chewed twice, then spit it out into the trash. "At least I won't have to worry about anybody coming to the party next year."

Trish planted her hands on her hips. "Dalton James, you did not just say that!"

"Kidding! I'm just kidding, of course." He kissed Trish on the top of the head, then looked at Sera and mouthed "no I'm not" before grimacing.

Sera giggled. She would let Trish explain that in the first batch they had forgotten to add the sugar to the sugar cookies, resulting in the heaping plate of rejects. Although the way Trish was looking at Dalton, she didn't think her cousin would be sharing that information any time soon.

Dalton started to leave the kitchen when Sera called out to him. He stopped and turned back to her. Sera swallowed several times, trying to get her suddenly dry throat to work. She finally took a quick drink of water, then cleared her throat.

"You need to give Andrew his job back."

Dalton stared at her for a moment, then glanced at his wife, who shrugged and focused on the dough she was mixing.

"He didn't do anything wrong." Sera was shocked by the boldness in her voice.

"That's for me to decide."

"No, it's not. I walked out on the ice and he saved me."

Dalton's face darkened. "He should never have let you walk out there in the first place."

Sera crossed her arms, refusing to give up. "You've met the women in my family." She threw a glance toward Trish, who was watching the volley and trying not to laugh. "When have you ever been able to control us—tell us what to do or what not to do?"

"She's got you there."

Dalton glared at his wife, then turned to walk out of the room.

Sera's shoulders slumped. She'd really thought she might be able to convince Dalton to rehire Andrew. She never considered that Dalton might simply refuse to listen to her. She looked at Trish and frowned. "I hope I didn't get you into any trouble."

"Nah." Trish shook her head.

Dalton returned, ushering Andrew into the kitchen. "Since you want him so badly, he's yours for the afternoon. That way I can take my wife to lunch."

"Heck yeah!" Trish threw her apron at Andrew. "Have fun, kiddos." She winked at Sera, then she and Dalton were gone.

Andrew stood frowning at Sera. "Told you I didn't need your help."

"Well, tough." She handed him a mixing bowl with all the ingredients for gingerbread cookies already added to it. "You got it anyway."

He set the bowl down on the counter. "No, I didn't."

Sera motioned for him to stir the mixture in the bowl.

Andrew rolled his eyes but complied. "He'd already hired me back, you know."

"Yeah, I know." She tasted the mixture in the bowl.

"You know, for such a smart woman, you sure are a horrible liar."

She stuck her tongue out at him. "Shut up and work."

Andrew dropped the wooden spoon in the bowl to offer her a proper military salute.

Sera pointed to the mixture. "I think that needs ginger still—or maybe vanilla? Something."

Andrew tasted a bit, smacking his lips loudly. "Tastes good to me."

"No." She shook her head, looking for the recipe card. "Something's off."

He chuckled. "Wow, you hate to be wrong, don't you?"

She stared at him, tapping her fingers on the counter. "We already screwed up one recipe. I don't want to mess up another one."

"It's fine. I swear." When she still didn't agree, he rolled his eyes. "Look, if the batch turns out bad, I'll eat them all myself. Okay?"

"All of them?"

"Every last one. Happy now?"

Sera glanced at the reject plate, noting just how many cookies one batch made. She stuck out her hand. "Deal."

Andrew shook her hand but didn't let go. "You think if I took a few classes at the community college up the road I could learn to be as good of a negotiator as you?"

Sera tried to pull her hand away, unsure if he was teasing her or not. He wouldn't let go. Instead he pulled her closer until she had to tilt her head back to look at him. He put one hand around her back to support her.

Sera felt her heart thumping in her chest. "I thought you said college was a waste of time." He was so close that if she stood on her tiptoes, their lips might meet.

He winced. "Uh, not so much a waste of time as I sort of lost my chance to go."

"Lost it?" She was willing his lips closer to hers. She opened her mouth just enough to signal to him that a kiss would be accepted. She would even return it. "Just make another chance."

"It's not that easy."

She smiled her best seductive smile. "Sure it is. You just call up and register. Or do it online."

"Some of us have jobs, responsibilities."

Sera licked her lips. "Sounds like a copout to me."

"It's reality." The corners of his lips turned down. She fought the desire to push them back up with her fingers.

"You shouldn't take college advice from me anyway."

"No? But I thought you knew all about higher education."

She was staring at his full, smooth lips. She knew she was, but couldn't look away. "Me? I don't know anything."

Suddenly he let go of her and stepped away, moving back to his mixing bowl, leaving Sera reeling.

"I told you not to do that."

She shook her head in confusion. "Do what?"

"Say you're dumb."

Sera curled her hands into fists. "I didn't say that." She ground out each word through clenched teeth.

"Don't know anything, dumb—same diff."

She tried to take a calming breath, but it didn't work. Instead, she grabbed one of the reject cookies, walked up to Andrew, and tapped him on the shoulder. When he turned to look at her, she shoved the cookie in his mouth. "You, sir, are an ass." Then she turned and calmly walked out of the kitchen, tossing back "and don't forget to clean up when you're done."

Chapter Eight

Andrew couldn't sleep. Something was up with Sera. She was hiding something, and it was driving him nuts not knowing what it was. That's why he couldn't sleep.

At least, that's what he told himself, even when he knew it wasn't the real reason.

Twice now he'd been close enough to kiss her—the kind of kiss that would make her head spin—but he'd screwed it up both times. The first time, in the parking lot, he'd chickened out. She had been cold or scared of him—or both—and he'd been afraid that she would reject him, plain and simple. Sera wouldn't offer a typical rejection, either. She'd do something unexpected, endearing, which would make the rejection that much more painful to swallow.

The second time, in the kitchen, he should have just shut up and kissed her. He knew she wanted to be kissed; he had seen her focused on his lips and felt her body relax into his. But he'd chosen that moment to bring up community college, apparently because he was a glutton for punishment. Her response had been the same line of thought she'd followed since arriving: degrading her intellect.

Andrew threw off the blankets and started pacing in his bedroom. What was it with her and college? Every time the subject came up, she made some comment to suggest that she wasn't as smart as he thought. It wasn't like he was equating her with Einstein, either. People went to college to get educated. It was why he'd wanted to go to college so badly, but when Lucas joined the army, Andrew had to put college on hold so he could cover the extra chores. By the time Lucas came home, there were medical bills and funeral arrangements for his wife. College just wasn't a priority anymore.

But for Sera, it was as if she didn't appreciate college, which rubbed Andrew the wrong way. More than that, she didn't seem to think she deserved to be in college. That was the part that was making him crazy—not the almost kisses or the way she wrinkled her nose when she laughed or the smell of lavender that followed her around.

He took a deep breath. That lavender smell was making him just as crazy. He was dying to know if it was from her soap or her shampoo or a body lotion. Whatever it was, it plagued his every waking thought.

Andrew glanced out the window and saw the barest hint of light touching the horizon. He'd waited long enough. He pulled on his jeans, then grabbed a thick sweater and headed downstairs.

He hung out in the Jameses' barn, waiting for some sign of life from the main house. The sun was already well above the horizon. He'd cleaned out the stalls, fed the horses, and taken the four-wheeler out for a tour of the property. Surely someone would be up by now. Most ranchers and farmers were up at the crack of dawn. Then again, Sera was neither of those, and he was damn sure didn't want to test Dalton again. He doubted Dalton would hire him a third time, no matter how much Trish and Sera begged.

He glanced at his phone. 7:54. He couldn't stand it anymore and headed for the front door.

As soon as he rang the doorbell, he decided he'd made a mistake. Dalton would answer the door and fire him on the spot. Or worse: Sera would answer and still be angry at him for the cookie fiasco. The night before, he had stayed in the kitchen until

Dalton and Trish returned several hours later, hoping that Sera would reappear. She hadn't. He'd baked all the cookies and cleaned up the kitchen, leaving it so spotless that Trish had asked about his rates for housecleaning.

The door swung open, and Andrew found himself staring at Sera. A smiling Sera. He let out the breath he'd been holding.

"Morning."

He nodded once, then quickly added, "Good morning."

She stood in the doorway, staring at him. "Can I help you with something?"

Trish called out from the hallway. "Lord, Sera, invite him in and close the door before you let all the heat out."

Sera nodded, then shuffled out onto the porch, pulling the door closed behind her.

"Sera." The warning in his voice was clear, but she held up a hand to stop him.

"I'll let you in on one condition: No talk of college or anything like that." She waited for him to comment, then finally said, "Deal?"

"Deal—on one condition of my own."

Sera rolled her eyes.

"You, missy, do not leave the house without proper winter clothing."

She glanced down at her sweater and jeans, then out to the porch. "Technically, I haven't left—"

"Uh-uh." He cut her off. "No 'technically.' No coat, no going outside."

"Fine." She turned to open the door, but it had locked behind her. She groaned, then rang the doorbell.

"And this would be why there is no 'technically' when it comes to wearing a coat."

Sera refused to look at him, but she couldn't stop herself from laughing. When Dalton opened the door, a bewildered look on his face, she laughed even harder, then pushed past him to get inside.

Dalton stood looking at Andrew. "You coming in?"

"Actually, I brought something." He motioned back to the four-wheeler, which had a large fir tree tied to the back.

Dalton's eyes narrowed, and Andrew quickly explained that he'd found it growing near the fence line. "You would've had to cut it next spring anyway."

"Did my wife put you up to this?"

Andrew shook his head.

Dalton walked down the porch steps. "Well, come on. Let's get it inside so you can make some major brownie points with Trish." He glanced over his shoulder. "Although I'm thinking that's not who you want to impress."

Andrew didn't look at Dalton as they untied the large tree and carried it inside. Trish's face lit up like a little kid's, and she clapped with excitement when she saw the tree. Sera's smile was more reserved, but Andrew didn't mind because she asked him to stay and help them decorate for the party. He hesitated, wondering why he hadn't thought his plan through.

Sera grabbed his hand and pulled him into the hallway. "I understand if you don't want to stay and help. I know Christmas can be hard when you're not with loved ones." She held his hand in both of hers, studying it. "But I really hope you'll stay." Finally, she looked up at him, flashed him a brilliant smile, then stood on her tiptoes and kissed his cheek before racing back into the living room to help with the tree.

Andrew smiled after her. Wild horses couldn't drag him away from her today.

Chapter Nine

Sera was nervous about the party. She focused her nervous energy in the kitchen, helping Trish put finger foods on different platters for Dalton to carry out to the living room. She giggled when she realized Dalton sampled each platter as he carried it. Trish gave him an exasperated sigh.

When the doorbell rang the first time, Sera nearly dropped the entire platter of deviled eggs. Luckily she managed to save it at the last minute, with a little help from Dalton.

"Relax. They're not all as intense as Lucas."

Sera smiled at him and tried to relax, but the realization that her nerves were showing made her even more nervous. So when Trish returned to the kitchen with Susannah Clark in tow, Sera's voice was so shrill she thought glass might shatter.

Susannah pulled Sera into a tight embrace, patting her back several times. When she stepped back, she winked. "Trust me. We're the ones who should be nervous meeting you."

"Huh?"

Susannah glanced at Trish. "Oh, you're right. She is a cutie. It all makes sense now." Susannah took Sera by the hand and led her out to the living room. "I'm just going to borrow her for a second, Trish. Better to do this in small doses."

Sera didn't understand what the woman was referring to, but her hazel eyes were kind, and Sera thought she might be able to relax. It didn't hurt that Susannah snatched a cup of eggnog off one of the trays and filled it with a healthy dose of rum before handing it to Sera. She took a tiny sip—just enough to taste the rum—then handed it back.

"Drink up, hon."

Sera blushed. "I'm not quite old enough yet. Legally, I mean."

Susannah nearly choked on the eggnog she was drinking.

"Annie, you okay?" A man with dark hair and olive skin walked up behind her and put his arm around her shoulders.

Susannah nodded. "Wrong pipe, that's all." She coughed a few more times before she could speak normally. "Tate, this is the famous Sera."

Sera stuck out her hand. "Serafina Anderson."

"Tate Trudell."

"Sheriff Tate Trudell," Susannah interjected.

Sera gave a sidelong glance to Susannah, unsure what to say next. They were saved when the doorbell rang again.

"Tate, sweetie, be a dear." Susannah waited for him to step away before grabbing Sera's arm. "Holy moly that was close. Being arrested by my fiancé on Christmas Eve—now that would be a story for the grandkids."

"Fiancé? Congrat—"

"Oh, no! Rats! He was right. I couldn't keep it secret." She glanced over her shoulder, where Tate was gathering coats from several people. Then she held up her hand to show off an intricately carved silver ring.

"It's gorgeous!"

"I know it's not your traditional diamond, but it's the perfect ring for us."

Trish appeared, crowding in close and signaling to Susannah to hand her a mug of eggnog. She waited while Susannah added rum. By the time she finished, Sera wondered if there was any nog left in the cup. Trish drank it back without stopping.

"Okay, that's my only one for the whole night." She nodded at Susannah's ring. "You showing her the ring? You can't keep a secret, can you?"

Susannah was practically giggling with excitement. "Well, she'll be heading home soon, so she doesn't really count, right?"

"Aunt Suz, look what I found!" A young girl ran over, Traitor close on her heels. She sat down on the floor next to him to rub his ears while he gave her puppy kisses. "Isn't he just the sweetest?"

"Jenny."

Sera recognized the powerful booming voice before she saw Lucas Clark. He was helping a gorgeous woman with platinum blond hair remove her coat.

Jenny sighed loudly as she stood up. "Yes, dad."

Trish linked arms with Sera. "Hope you're ready for this."

Sera looked at her cousin, her knees suddenly quite weak.

Trish smiled and patted her hand. "I'm joking. You'll be fine." When Lucas and the woman entered the living room, Trish hugged each of them, then introduced Sera to Miranda.

"Dalton's sister Miranda?" Sera asked, the shock evident in her voice. "You don't look anything alike." Sera raised her hand to her mouth as soon as she realized what she'd said.

Miranda smiled and leaned in as if sharing a secret. "Different mothers."

"But both with the same bull-headedness," Trish said.

"Amen to that," Lucas chimed in. He winked at Miranda, who rolled her eyes playfully, then turned to Trish. "Daniel and Jonathan send their apologies. They're both spending the evening with their girlfriends' families."

Trish squeezed Sera's hand. "Well, then we're all here. See? That wasn't so bad."

Sera took a deep breath. She would only have to deal with two of Andrew's siblings tonight, one of whom she already knew. She smiled, feeling much more in the Christmas spirit.

The doorbell rang again. Sera shot out of the living room, calling out "I'll get it" over her shoulder. She threw open the door, then tapped her foot and pointed to an imaginary watch. "Were you planning on leaving me here to fend off your family all by myself?"

Andrew chuckled as he stepped through the door. Sera caught a whiff of a crisp, slightly musky smell with hints of vanilla. She leaned in close and inhaled deeply. Andrew raised an eyebrow in question.

"Just enjoying the holiday smells." She winked at him, then motioned toward the living room.

"Hey, Uncle Andrew."

"Hey, munchkin." He reached out to tousle Jenny's hair, but she pulled back.

"Um, really? I'm ten now. Too old to be a munchkin." She stuck her tongue out, then looked over her shoulder nervously to see if anyone had witnessed the act. Sera covered her mouth to prevent herself from laughing.

Dalton appeared from the kitchen, licking his fingers as he passed through the hall. He spied Jenny and stopped. "Well, well. I do believe I've caught someone under the mistletoe." He pointed to a small bunch of mistletoe hung from the entryway into the living room. "That means I get a kiss."

Jenny looked up at the mistletoe, studying it, then drew an imaginary line straight down from it, stopping on Traitor's head. "Yep, you're right. You get a kiss from Traitor." She turned and raced back into the living room.

Dalton clapped Andrew on the shoulder. "She's gonna break a lot of hearts. A lot of hearts!" He motioned for Sera and Andrew to follow him into the living room, but then stopped just after he crossed into the room and spun around to smile at them. "Now it's your turn under the mistletoe."

Sera felt butterflies in her stomach as she turned to Andrew, but he was already bending down to kiss her cheek. Before she enjoy the moment, he had pushed his way into the living room and was talking to his brother. She tried to hide her disappointment with such an innocent kiss, but her smile felt fake. So when Trish asked Dalton to bring in another tray of cheese and crackers, Sera didn't hesitate to offer to go instead. Thankfully, Dalton didn't argue with her.

When she returned, she handed the platter to Trish just as the doorbell rang. "Don't worry, I'll get it." *Anything to avoid being in the same room with Andrew right now.* She assumed that one of his brothers had decided to come after all, so when she opened the door, her plastered-on smile faltered.

"Mom? Dad? What are you doing here?"

Chapter Ten

Andrew turned to see what everyone was staring at. A hush fell over the living room, which was quickly replaced with squeals coming from the hallway. He saw Sera standing at the door, one hand gripping the doorknob so tightly he thought she might rip it off. The squeals were not coming from her.

A tall woman, dressed elegantly in a full-length silver fur coat, stepped inside, followed by an equally tall man with a head full of thick black hair. The woman grabbed Sera, hugging her tightly as they rocked back and forth.

The man placed a hand on the woman's shoulder. "Let her breathe, Lydia. We didn't fly all this way only to suffocate her."

Trish pushed through the people in the living room. "Wilson? Lydia?" She glanced at Dalton and whispered, "Sera's parents."

"Sera? Oh, what is that? Your name is Serafina." Lydia frowned at Trish. "Honestly, why you girls feel the need to ruin everything we give you—and what have you done to your hair, young lady?"

Sera tucked the swath of blue behind her ear and studied her feet.

Wilson cleared his throat loudly, closing the door behind him. "Sweetie, now is not the time."

Lydia looked at Sera, then grabbed her in another hug. "Oh, you're right. I get to see my Serafina again. That's all that matters."

Andrew watched Sera closely. She was going through the motions, but her face was as white as a sheet. Something was wrong, but he wasn't sure he should intervene. This was her family, after all. He moved a bit closer to the entryway, willing Sera to look his way. Maybe if she saw him, she could make some gesture, do something to let him know she was all right.

"What are you doing here?" Sera's voice was hesitant, but Andrew was apparently the only one who noticed—or the only one who cared. The thought made him bristle in indignation.

"Honestly, Serafina. What a silly question." Lydia slid her coat off and handed it to her husband. "We're here to celebrate Christmas with you."

"But...Rome. You're supposed to be—"

"Your mother couldn't stand the thought of celebrating Christmas without you. No matter how much it cost me in last-minute airfare."

Lydia turned to her husband and pursed her lips. "Hush. It's Christmas." She looked at the room full of guests watching everything unfold in the hallway. "Well, now. Who do we have here?"

Trish made the introductions, and everyone found a place to sit. Only Sera remained standing in the doorway, her face still ashen. Andrew motioned for her to come sit next to him on the couch, but she didn't notice. All her attention was on her parents, and it was clear that she was not happy to see them. She looked downright terrified in fact.

"It's so nice to meet you all." Lydia held up a glass of eggnog. "And a toast. To all of you for welcoming Serafina to your celebration this year."

Everyone drank to the toast except Sera, Andrew, and Jenny, who was sitting on the floor with Traitor.

Lydia finished off her entire glass of eggnog, then dabbed at her lips as she looked around. "This really is a quaint little home you have here, Trish."

"Mother!"

Miranda choked on her eggnog, and Dalton's brown eyes darkened with anger. Only Trish remained unflappable.

"Thank you, Lydia. It's still a work in progress, but it's our home and it's perfect for us."

"I do hope that Serafina hasn't been too much trouble."

Trish smiled. "None at all. We've loved having her." She glanced at Sera. "Hopefully it won't be another decade before she comes to visit again."

"I know. This child is such a busy one, what with school and all." Lydia clasped her hands and beamed with pride at her daughter. "But it will all be worth it once she gets through med school."

Everyone looked at Sera, who seemed to shrink even further into the hallway.

"Med school?" Susannah sat up straighter. "As in a medical doctor?"

Lydia let loose a musical laugh. "Oh, heaven's no. Seraphina will be a psychiatrist."

Andrew felt as if he'd been doused in ice-cold water. He slowly turned to stare at Sera, who glanced at him repeatedly, as if afraid to look at him but still wanting to see his reaction. He started to rise from the sofa. Dalton tried to pull him back down, but Andrew shook him off. He was focused only on Sera now, only on how she lied to him.

"Sera, be a dear and check on the dinner in the oven." Trish's voice was shaky. Sera nodded, then bolted for the kitchen. "Andrew could you—?"

But Andrew was already following Sera down the hallway. He barged through the door to find her pacing in front of the counter, mumbling to herself.

Andrew sneered. "Now that's rich."

Sera looked up at him, confused.

"Mumbling to yourself, as if you've gone off the deep end. Is that something you learned in your psych program?" He slapped his forehead. "Oh, wait. That's right. You couldn't get into that one. Well, that's what you told me." He took a step closer. "Bet you thought it was a hoot, pretending not to know about PTSD. Why was that? Trying to make the ignorant country boy feel smart? Some experiment you decided to carry out?"

"It's not like that," Sera hissed.

"Whatever, Sera—oh, I mean, Serafina." He rolled his eyes in disgust. "Even your name's a lie."

"I wasn't lying—I didn't lie to you!"

"Whatever." He turned to leave, but she grabbed his arm and spun him back around.

"No, you don't get to walk away from me. Not like this."

He bent down and jabbed his finger at her. "You don't own me. I'm not some servant you can boss around."

"Oh, my God. You think we have servants?" She threw back her head and laughed.

"Is that another lie?"

Sera glared at him now. "Andrew Clark, stop being a pig-headed jerk. I wasn't lying. I couldn't get into the program because I flunked out of college."

Andrew started to accuse her of lying again, but something stopped him. He thought back to her comments the last several days, comments that related to her not being smart enough.

"Young lady, what do you mean you flunked out?"

Sera and Andrew turned to see her father standing in the doorway, an angry frown on his face.

"Oh, hell."

"Language!"

Sera sank into a chair by the table. "Oh, daddy, give it a rest. I say a lot worse than hell."

Wilson exchanged an uncomfortable look with Andrew. "If you don't mind, I think I need to speak with my daughter in private."

Andrew looked at Sera, who nodded. He started to walk past Wilson, but the older man stuck a hand out to stop him.

"You care about her?"

Andrew could barely hear the words. He nodded without hesitating.

"Then do me a favor and don't mention any of this to her mother."

Andrew nodded once again, then walked out of the kitchen.

Chapter Eleven

Sera was afraid to look at her father, a man whose very presence intimidated even the most self-assured person. It wasn't just his height. His piercing eyes were always quick to get to the heart of the matter. Tonight she was sure those eyes would be full of disappointment directed solely at her.

After several minutes of uncomfortable silence, she finally peeked up at him.

"So tell me about the boy."

Her head snapped up in surprise, but in the next moment she was looking down once again, this time studying her hands and rubbing at an imaginary speck of dirt.

"So you do like him."

"Not that it matters now," she mumbled. "He hates me."

Her father pulled her into a tight hug, and she could feel his chest rumbling with laughter. "Trust your old man on this one. That boy has it bad for you."

She sank into his hug, enjoying the comfort it provided while letting her mind explore the idea of Andrew liking her. She certainly was attracted to him and his gruff social skills. And technically, she didn't have to leave after the holidays…

She started to pull away from her father. "Daddy, I—"

"Don't worry. It's Christmas. Nothing we can do about school tonight, so let's just save this discussion until the day after Christmas. Consider it my gift to you."

She hugged him tightly once more.

When they walked back into the living room, her mother was droning on about Rome.

"Come along, Lydia. Why don't we head to our hotel and let these young people celebrate on their own?"

Her mother stood and offered profuse thanks while her husband helped her into her coat. "Come along, Serafina."

"Sera's going to stay here tonight." Wilson led his wife to the front door before his wife could protest.

"Come on, sweetie. A night all to ourselves in a tiny hotel? It'll be like our honeymoon."

"And I'll be over for Christmas morning with you. I promise." Sera nodded in encouragement as she sank onto the couch next to Andrew.

Everyone in the living room waited silently, listening as Sera's parents drove away in their rental car. Only when the sound of the engine could no longer be heard did they relax, seeming to let out a collective sigh.

"So those were my parents..." Sera plastered a fake smile on her face, causing everyone to laugh. Just like that, the tension was gone, and the party was once again in full swing. Sera grabbed Andrew's hand and squeezed it. When she started to pull away, he grabbed her hand and squeezed back. And he didn't let go.

"Time for presents!" Trish waved for Jenny to come help her hand out gifts.

Sera couldn't stop smiling as she watched everyone get excited about the finely wrapped boxes being handed to them.

Andrew leaned over to whisper in her ear. "So everything okay with your dad?"

She nodded. "It will be. College just isn't for me—especially not eight more years of it."

Andrew frowned.

"What's the matter?"

He shook his head. "Nothing."

Before Sera could protest, Jenny dropped a brightly colored box in Andrew's lap. "You must have been really good this year because Santa apparently brought you something." Andrew turned the gift over in his hands, then read the tag.

Sera pointed at the box. "I hope you won't be offended that I got you a little something. I promise it didn't contribute too much to the capitalists or the fat man."

He ripped into the wrapping paper like a little boy, making it hard for Sera not to laugh at him. Inside was a bright yellow mug with blue writing that said "World's Greatest Teacher." He held it up, his brow furrowing in confusion.

Sera leaned over and whispered, "Look inside."

He tilted the mug forward and dug out the keychain inside. On the end was a small four-wheeler. He chuckled, then threw an arm around her and pulled her into a hug. He kissed her forehead. "It's perfect."

"So you don't have it already?"

He laughed even harder. "No, this is certainly a unique gift." He looked down at her. "Meaningful."

Sera stared up at him, wondering if he would finally kiss her. But Susannah interrupted their moment, and he loosened his hold on Sera so he could show Susannah the mug and keychain.

Susannah looked at Sera. "So what did he get you?" She glanced at Andrew. "You're kidding. You didn't get her anything?" She slapped him on the shoulder. "Are you really that dense?"

"It's okay." Sera pointed at the mug. "I didn't really get him anything—it was more of a joke, really. Right?" She nodded at Andrew, telling herself to keep her face calm and show no emotion. Inside, however, she was devastated. She told herself that it was all a part of who Andrew was. He didn't like Christmas, didn't support gift-giving, and she should be okay with that. She could certainly understand his stance on the consumerism part of the holiday.

But she couldn't ignore the hurt that was welling up inside her. She stood up, tossed out a small "excuse me," then fled to the kitchen before her tears spilled over for everyone to see. She grabbed a paper towel and blotted at her eyes, telling herself it was stupid to cry. Andrew had made it clear that he didn't celebrate Christmas, so why had she hoped that he would somehow be different with her? Standing by the sink, she took several deep breaths, then ran cold water over her hands and held them to her cheeks. When she finally thought she was calm enough to return to the living room, she turned around.

Andrew was standing behind her, watching her. He stepped forward, reaching up to run a thumb under her eye. He stared into her eyes for what seemed like an eternity.

"I did get you something."

Sera swallowed, wondering if she'd heard him correctly. "Huh?"

He stepped back and pulled a small flat item about the size of a playing card from his pocket. It was wrapped it wrinkled blue paper. "I did get you something, but now I think it's the wrong thing—"

Sera placed her hand over his.

"Sera..."

"You got this—for me?"

He nodded.

"But now you don't want to give it to me?"

"No, I—I want to, but I think after everything tonight...maybe it's the wrong time."

Sera frowned. "Is it a warrant for my arrest?"

Andrew laughed and dropped his chin to his chest. "No."

She reached out to lift his chin until he was looking in her eyes. "It's fine. Whatever it is, when you're ready, so am I."

The muscles in his jaw twitched, and she could tell he was weighing the pro and the cons.

"Okay." He exhaled slowly. "Open it."

"You sure?"

He shoved it at her. "Quick, quick. Before I change my mind."

She carefully pulled at the tape, afraid that she would pull more than wrapping paper. Inside, she found a folded up piece of paper. When she opened it and read it, she gasped.

She couldn't stop smiling. "Are you serious?"

"You're not upset?"

"Upset? Of course not—I'm proud of you for making new chances."

She stared up at him, and their eyes locked. The noises the from the other room disappeared as the world around them seemed to shrink until it was just the two of them. Sera was convinced she could hear his heart beating in time to her own. *Now! Kiss me now!*

The spell was broken when Trish stepped into the kitchen carrying several empty platters. "Oops, sorry. Didn't mean to interrupt."

Sera clumsily looked away, then realized she was still holding the paper Andrew gave her. "Look at this—look what he did."

Sera handed the paper to Trish, who read it, then whistled. "Animal science, plant science—those you won't have any problems with at all. Heck, you could even teach the classes." She handed the paper back to Andrew. "Agribusiness degree?"

Andrew nodded.

"Good move. If you need to know which teachers to avoid, let me know. I just finished my degree there last year." She headed back for the door, then stopped. "They've got a pretty good liberal arts program, Sera. In case you're interested." She was gone before Sera could respond.

Andrew turned to Sera. "She's right, you know."

Sera held up her hands. "No, no, this girl is done with college. At least for a while."

"So what are you going to do?"

She thought for a moment. "I'd really like to explore my creative side, maybe learn to draw."

Andrew slid an arm around her waist. "I might be able to help with that."

"Oh, so you're an artist now, too?"

"Me?" He snorted. "No way. But my brother is—and he's dating a professional artist."

Sera glanced at the door. "Who, Lucas?"

"No, Jonathan. You'll meet him soon."

"Well, then maybe I'll have to talk to Trish about renting out a room for a bit."

"Maybe you will."

They stared at each other, smiling.

"Oh!" Andrew dug in his pocket. "I almost forgot. I have something else for you." He pulled out a badly bruised sprig of mistletoe.

"It's about time!" Sera reached up to pull him down in a kiss—and this time, it was no peck on the cheek.

Acknowledgments

Oh, to be back in college (or at least college age)! That was a time when we were fearless and free—a daring and always invigorating combination. I won't bore you with my escapades from that time (I'll save them for another book), but I will say thanks to my college roommate, Katie Beckner Parsons, for not only surviving my antics but also coming up with plenty of her own (hello, Cleveland?!). I also want to thank Kerry Cooper, who continues to have exciting adventures every day. To Katie and Kerry, my deepest thanks for reminding me that life is meant to be lived every single day.

Turn the page for a sneak peek at

Vibrant Heart

Book 1 in the Great Plains Romance Series

Melanie Olson swore under her breath and pulled the rented Ford Fusion onto the shoulder of the barely paved country road. She was already running late thanks to a delayed flight. Now a flat tire?

She got out of the car, her high heels sinking into the soft Nebraska dirt along the shoulder, and found the culprit: the rear passenger-side wheel. Looking at it more closely, she saw a nail as thick as her thumb stuck in the tire.

"Just great," she muttered. Glancing around, she noted the storm clouds moving in quickly from the west. The road, however, was deserted. "Naturally." She opened the trunk to dig out the spare. "All dressed up and actually in a position to use my feminine wiles for once in my life and not a single taker. Typical!"

She was only a few miles from her parents' house—no, check that, her father's house. She thought about calling for some help but tossed that idea aside. It was already time for the ceremony to start, and she couldn't interrupt the nuptials just because she wasn't dressed to change a tire. Knowing her luck, her dad would send Raymond out to help her. Her frown deepened. Being stranded and helpless was not the impression she planned for him.

She pulled out her weekend bag and set it on the ground next to the car, followed by her laptop and the wedding gift: a large crystal punchbowl. She smiled as she pulled back the flooring of the truck to reveal the spare tire and jack kit. The punchbowl was certainly beautiful, but its significance wouldn't be lost on her father. A shattered punchbowl had been the final straw, causing her mother to leave him.

Melanie focused on loosening the lug nuts. She was not a tiny girl by any stretch of the imagination. She looked most men in the eye and had enough meat on her that they didn't mistake her for some starving waif. But she wasn't a body builder, and she was beginning to think whoever attached the tire was. No matter how much she strained, the lug nut wouldn't budge. She redoubled her efforts, anxious to get the tire changed before the storm broke. She wouldn't have even bothered to come back for her father's wedding except she knew Raymond would be there, and she wanted to flaunt her new position as executive editor at GPP Press. Getting her hair cut and highlighted as well as finding the pale lavender dress that accentuated her curves in all the right ways would make it all the easier to remind him of what he had given up—and she couldn't wait to rub his nose in it.

The lug nut still wouldn't budge. This would not do at all. Calling her dad for help because she had a flat tire would be humiliating enough. Telling him she wasn't strong enough to remove the flat? Icing on the cake. Dammit! She was not going to let this stupid tire ruin her plans. She grabbed the bar and pressed against it with all her weight. The lug nut finally gave way, releasing against the pressure and sending her sprawling to the ground.

Her knees and palms were scraped and raw, her pale dress streaked with dirt, but Melanie didn't care. She had gotten the first lug nut loosened. It would all be downhill from here.

Then she felt the first raindrops, fat drops that plopped heavily into the dirt around her. Everything was still sitting out next to the rental car, and she scrambled to get her laptop and luggage stuffed into the backseat.

By the time she returned to fixing the tire, the rain was coming down so hard that her dress was plastered to her body and her dark hair clung to her face and neck. She tried to loosen the second lug nut, but her wet hands couldn't get any traction. The nut wouldn't budge.

"Are you freaking kidding me?" she screamed. So much for showing off to Raymond. She probably looked like a drowned rat. If she even made it to the ceremony in time—which was looking doubtful at this point—and Raymond was still there, he'd be heaving a sigh of relief instead of kicking himself for letting her get away. Of course, she probably wasn't going to see him anyway because she was stuck on the side of the road in an early afternoon thunderstorm.

"This is why I hate coming back here!" she yelled over the rain. "This. Right here!"

"Hey, darlin', you need some help?"

Melanie spun around to find a man standing in front of a classic Chevy pickup parked several yards back, its dim lights shining on her trunk. The man's broad shoulders—the kind that said he wasn't afraid of hard work—were hunched up under his cowboy hat. His denim shirt was wet enough that Mel could see the muscles working under it, and she had to admit, she definitely approved. But it was when she looked up into his face that her heartbeat went all erratic. His rich green eyes seemed to sparkle, even though the sun was hidden behind thick rain clouds, and the corners of his mouth curled up slightly in a perpetual smile. She fought the urge to run her hand along his jawline and trace the outline of his bottom lip with her thumb.

"Help?" Melanie cleared her throat. She chastised herself for getting all woozy over this cowboy, which was clearly not on the schedule. Suddenly furious that help hadn't shown up ten minutes earlier, she snapped, "No, I actually like standing here in the rain, *darlin'*."

The man pushed by her to the spare tire, turning his face away slightly, but Melanie still saw him laughing.

"Why don't you go sit in my truck where it's dry...darlin'." Melanie could tell he added the "darlin'" as an afterthought.

He loosened the nuts holding the spare as if they melted under his touch, and Melanie wanted to throw the nuts on the ground and stomp on the small, traitorous chunks of metal that were so pliable under his touch. Of course, who could blame them?

"How do I know you aren't some psycho who goes around stealing women from the side of the road?" Melanie snapped at him as he hefted the spare out of the trunk, the denim shirt pulling tightly against his arms and shoulders. He set the spare on the bumper, then turned to Melanie and smiled. Melanie leaned against the car for support as she drank in his strong jawline and emerald eyes. She half wished that he would steal her, take her into his truck, and let her press her body against his.

"Psychos don't actually change the tires before stealing the women, now do they, darlin'?"

And just like that, the spell was broken. He jacked up the car while Melanie gritted her teeth.

"Please don't call me that."

He moved to the far side of the car while Melanie stood by the trunk, waiting. She wished she could sit in her own car while he was changing the tire and dry off a little bit. She certainly wasn't going to sit in his truck. Luckily the rain started letting up. Although it didn't stop, it was certainly more tolerable.

"Now I never did get why women don't like being called that." He stood up to put the flat into the trunk.

Melanie just looked at him.

"'Darlin', I mean." He closed the trunk and leaned against the back of the car.

Melanie snorted. "Because it's belittling. And patronizing. And sexist," she said, crossing her arms. "Not that I expect you to understand that."

He took a step to walk past her, stopping just as they were shoulder to shoulder. "But a beautiful woman stranded in the rain on the side of the road? That's just damn sexy."

His husky laugh gave her goose bumps.

"I said sexist, not sexy!"

He was already climbing into his truck, watching her and laughing.

Melanie scampered into her car. She scowled into the rearview mirror, waiting for him to take off, but he just sat in his truck, waiting, which infuriated her even more. She rolled down her window and waved for him to go on by her. He didn't move.

"Fine, jerk," she mumbled under her breath as she rolled up the window. She put the car into gear and pulled onto the road, trying to ignore the hint of disappointment she felt because she wouldn't get to press her body against his after all.

Books in the Great Plains Romance Series

Vibrant Heart

When the ever-organized Melanie Olson returns to her small Nebraska hometown to prove to the commitment-phobe Raymond what a mistake he made, a flat tire threatens to ruin all her plans. Luckily, cowboy-turned-entrepreneur Jake Monroe stops to help the woman stranded by the side of the road, unaware that his world is about to be turned on end. Realizing that she's traveling to the same wedding he is, he decides fate has dealt him a winning hand—until he discovers that she only has eyes for the town womanizer. Jake is determined to get the beautiful spitfire to look his way, but her intensity might be too much for even him to handle.

A Heart's Promise

Trish Cassidy is an easygoing woman with a goal: to manage her own ranch. But after her parents' death, she finds herself stuck with a dominating boyfriend who has probably just ruined her last chance to connect with the local ranchers. Just when she thinks she must give up on her dream, the enigmatic Dalton James steps into her life, offering an opportunity to build a ranch from the ground up. What she doesn't expect is her powerful attraction to her new boss—or how controlling he starts to become.

When Dalton James decided to build his horse ranch, the last thing he anticipated was saving a damsel in distress. Then again, Trish Cassidy isn't someone who needs saving. So why is he so protective of her? More importantly, why does he feel like he has to do the right thing around her, even when she doesn't want him to?

Heart So Sweet

With four older brothers, rancher Susannah Clark is used to dealing with men and getting them out of trouble. But when her childhood crush Tate Trudell returns as sheriff of Harrington County, Susannah must decide whether to save her brothers yet again, even if means losing the man she loves.

Tate Trudell never expected to move back to Harrington, especially after how he left things with his best friend, Lucas Clark, just before Lucas left for the war in Afghanistan. But a lot has changed in ten years, including Susannah, Lucas' little sister. When Tate discovers that her passion matches his own, he's determined to be with her. To get the woman of his dreams, he must work through his bad blood with the Clark family—if Lucas doesn't kill him first.

So Wills the Heart

When the tough gets going, artist Evie Jacobson runs away. So when her great aunt leaves her a property in rural Nebraska, Evie uses the opportunity to escape her boss, who's deluded himself into thinking she loves him. But life in the country is a bit too tame for Evie—until she meets Jonathan Clark, a man who tests the limits of her spontaneity. When Evie discovers that Jonathan might not be everything she expected, will she runaway yet again or will she have the strength to stay and face her greatest test?

Jonathan Clark's afternoon break from working the ranch turns into a fantasy-come-to-life when he encounters Evie Jacobson skinny dipping in a private pond. His water nymph's playful side excites him like no woman he's ever met, and he looks for any excuse to be with her. But a rancher's work is never done, and Jonathan must choose between his family and Evie—a woman who might have already moved on to someone else.

My Heart, My Gift

Can the big city girl convince the small-town cowboy to give Christmas a second chance? Or will the secret she hides destroy any chance of a relationship between them?

When Serafina Anderson makes a mess of her first semester of college, she does what she knows best: avoids facing her parents. This time she runs away to spend her winter vacation at the ranch of her cousin, Trish. Her escapades also lead her right into the arms of Andrew Clark, the small town's most notorious troublemaker. But Sera sees beyond Andrew's crass nature and recognizes that the bad boy isn't as bad as everyone makes him out to be.

Andrew Clark hates Christmas—at least he has since his parents died. He refuses to buy into the commercialism of the holiday and does his best to shove the hurt he feels down so deep inside him that no one will ever find it. So when Sera ignores his bad temper and rude remarks, he wonders if he's finally found the angel who can rescue him from himself—until he discovers that she's been lying to him all along.

About the Author

Corrissa James was not always a country girl. In fact, she fought it all her life, traveling the world to live in far-flung cities like St. Petersburg, Russia, Caracas, Venezuela, Varanasi, India, and Guadalajara, Mexico. She didn't realize she was meant to live in the country until she returned to her roots in Nebraska, where she discovered the beauty of the fields around her (even if she was allergic to them) and the intensity of Mother Nature (who sure packs a wallop!).

Corrissa wrote her first romance stories in junior high, although at the time she didn't really know what happened after kissing, so she improvised with lots of ellipses (…). Her professional writing career initially took her away from romance—but never far away as Corrissa could always be found with a romance book at hand.

Today she focuses on western romance novellas, offering afternoon reads focused on strong women and the men they choose (never without some struggles along the way).

If you've enjoyed this book, please leave a review.

Thank you!

Check out more works by Corrissa James and see
what's coming next by visiting
www.corrissajames.com